There's a Hole in My Pocket

Based on a Traditional American Song

Adapted by Akimi Gibson
Pictures by Jeni Bassett

SCHOLASTIC INC.

New York   Toronto   London   Auckland   Sydney

Copyright © 1994 by Scholastic Inc.
All rights reserved. Published by Scholastic Inc.
Printed in the U.S.A.
ISBN 0-590-27598-4

16 15 14   00 99 98

There's a hole in my pocket.

Fix it.

How can I fix it?

Sew it.

How do I sew it?

With a needle and thread.

How can I get them?

Buy them.

How do I buy them?

With money.

Well, how can I carry it?

In your pocket.

But there's a hole in my pocket!